Based on the series created by
CHRIS NEE

Special thanks to
TANYA REMER ALTMANN, MD FAPP
for her contributions to this story

First Edition 10 9 8 7 6 5 4 3 2 1
ISBN 978-1-4231-8390-7
F322-8368-0-14206
Library of Congress Control Number: 2014936381

Printed in the USA

Visit disneybooks.com

# Doc McStuffins
# Doctor's Helper

Written by
SHEILA SWEENY
HIGGINSON

Illustrated by
MIKE WALL

Disney PRESS
New York • Los Angeles

Doc McStuffins is having the best game of hide-and-seek ever. "Ready or not, here I come!" she calls to her toys.

"Oh, we're ready, Doc!" Stuffy yells from behind the slide.

"Stuffy, shhh!" Lambie whispers. "Doc is not supposed to find us."

"Is it okay that *I* found something hiding?" Chilly asks.

Doc walks over to take a look.
Stuffy and Lambie go over, too.

They all want to know what Chilly found.

They spy something long and curvy behind him.

It's **not** a dragon tail. It's **not** a jump rope. It's a **trunk** . . . and that trunk belongs to . . .

a toy elephant!

"I asked her name," Chilly says. "But she didn't answer."

Doc picks up the little elephant. "Can you tell me your name?" she asks.

The elephant tries to answer, but she can't. Her shoulders start to shake. She waves her trunk in the air.

Doc hears her sneezing and wheezing, too.

"That doesn't sound very good," says Doc.

Stuffy, Lambie, and Chilly lean in closely.

"I hear it, too, Doc!" Stuffy says.
"She's trying to talk, but she can't."

"Don't worry," Lambie says.
"You're lucky we found you.
Doc is the best at fixing toy
troubles!"

"How will we know who she belongs to if she can't talk to us?" Chilly wonders.

"First we'll take her to the clinic and find out what's wrong," Doc says. "Then we'll figure out how to get her back where she belongs."

Doc and her toys head to the clinic.

"Hallie," Doc says. "We found this little elephant in the park, and something's not right."

It's time for a checkup!

"Howdy-do, sugar," Hallie says cheerfully.
"I'm as happy as a hog at a hoedown to meet you."

"My . . . name . . . isn't . . . Sugar," the elephant
gasps. "It's . . . **Ellie**."

Doc takes Ellie into the examination room.

She uses her stethoscope to listen to Ellie's trunk and chest.

Ellie's shoulders start to shake again.

"Ellie, don't take this the wrong way,"
says Hallie. "But you're wheezier than
a walrus with a whiny whistle."

"I know you're upset, Ellie," Doc says. "But I think that's making your wheezing worse."

"Lambie, I have an important job for you," says Doc. "Would you give Ellie a cuddle while I check her?"

"Of course!" Lambie replies. "One cuddle coming right up!"

"Do you have any jobs for a brave dragon?" Stuffy wonders.

"As a matter of fact, I do, Stuffy," Doc replies. "You could hold Ellie's hand to help her stay calm."

Ellie breathes **in** . . .

and **out.**

**In** . . .

and **out.**

Finally, she starts to relax.

"Ellie, I'm going to look inside your trunk," Doc says.
"I want to see what's making it so stuffy and sneezy.
That might be why you're wheezing, too. My cousin
starts to wheeze whenever she's near a cat."

"I hope she's not allergic to dragons!" Stuffy cries.

Ellie shakes her head and smiles at Stuffy.

No dragon allergies for this little elephant!

Then Doc shines a light inside Ellie's trunk.

**"Aha!"** she says. "I see what the problem is!"

"Ellie, you have a case of STUFFY-TRUNK-ATOSIS,"
Doc explains.

She writes her diagnosis in

The BIG BOOK of
BOO-BOOS.

"Stuffy-what-a-whose-is?"
Stuffy stammers. "I hope she
didn't get it from me!"

"No, Stuffy," Doc laughs. "Stuffy-**TRUNK**-atosis. It just means there's a lot of dust and dirt inside Ellie's trunk. It was windy in the park, so it must have blown in there."

"That sounds serious," says Stuffy.

"Don't worry, Stuffy," Doc says. "We'll fix Ellie up and she'll be fine."

Doc grabs a special tool.

"I'm going to use this to rinse the dust and dirt out of your trunk," she says. "And I promise, it won't hurt a bit."

Ellie squeezes Stuffy's hands a little tighter.

Stuffy squeezes back and tries to look even braver.

When Doc is finished, Ellie says, "Thank you! I feel so much better now."

"Then why do I still see tears, honey?" Hallie wonders.

"I have to find Sam," Ellie says sadly.

"I'm more than just Sam's toy. I'm a doctor's helper, too," she explains.

"Sam has allergies and asthma. Asthma makes it hard to breathe sometimes, so I remind Sam to take long, slow breaths."

"What's Sam like?" Stuffy asks.
"Maybe I can fly around and do a search."

"You can't really fly, Stuffy," Lambie
reminds him. "You're a toy."

Looking
for
Owner
freckles
red hair
6 years old
Sam

"Stuffy's right, though," Doc says.
"Tell us all about Sam so we know
who to look for."

Ellie tells them everything she can remember.
Lambie, Stuffy, and the other toys get to work.

Looking
for
Owner
freckles
red hair
6 years old
Sam

"Breathe easy, Ellie," Doc whispers.
"We'll find Sam soon."

Doc heads back to the playground the next morning.

After all the posters are hung, Doc looks around for Sam.

She sees a boy with red hair on the slide and races over to him.

He **isn't** Sam.

She spots a girl with freckles
jumping rope and runs over to her.

She **isn't** Sam, either.

"What if we never find Sam?" Chilly cries.

"Take a deep breath, Chilly," says Ellie.

"Ellie's right," Doc agrees. "Breathe easy.
We have to find Sam, and we will."

Suddenly, Doc notices a grown-up looking at one of the posters!
"Everyone go stuffed!" she whispers to the toys.

A girl with red hair and freckles is looking at the poster, too.

Doc wheels her wagon over to the girl.

Looking
for
Owner
freckles
red hair
6 years old
Sam

She **is** Sam!

"I think I found your elephant,"
Doc says to the girl.

Looking
for
Owner
freckles
red hair
6

"Ellie!"

Sam shouts happily.

"Thank you!

Thank you!

Thank you!"

"Thank you for finding Ellie," Sam says. "I thought she was lost forever!"

"You're welcome," Doc replies.

"Now that Ellie and Sam are back together, I can finally breathe easy," says Chilly.

"You really are the best at fixing toy troubles, Doc," Lambie says.

"And lost owner troubles, too!" Hallie adds. "Good work, Doc!"

"Thanks, but I couldn't have done it without all of you," Doc says. "You're the best doctor's helpers ever!"

# WHAT PARENTS AND CAREGIVERS SHOULD KNOW ABOUT ALLERGIES AND ASTHMA

Allergies affect as many as 40 percent of children and are one of the many triggers of asthma.

Asthma is one of the most common chronic childhood diseases. Currently, about one in ten children in the United States suffers from asthma.

Asthma attacks can turn serious quickly, so it's important that both parents and child know the child's asthma triggers and work together to stay away from them. Well-controlled allergies and asthma shouldn't stop children from participating in the activities they love.

- Keep your child's allergies and asthma well controlled with daily preventive medication, and keep rescue medicine close by just in case.

- For dust mite allergies, wash sheets, blankets, and mattresses once a week and dry completely.

- During pollen season, try to keep windows closed and bathe after playing outside.

- Make an asthma plan and share it with all your child's caregivers, including babysitters, teachers, and daycare workers.